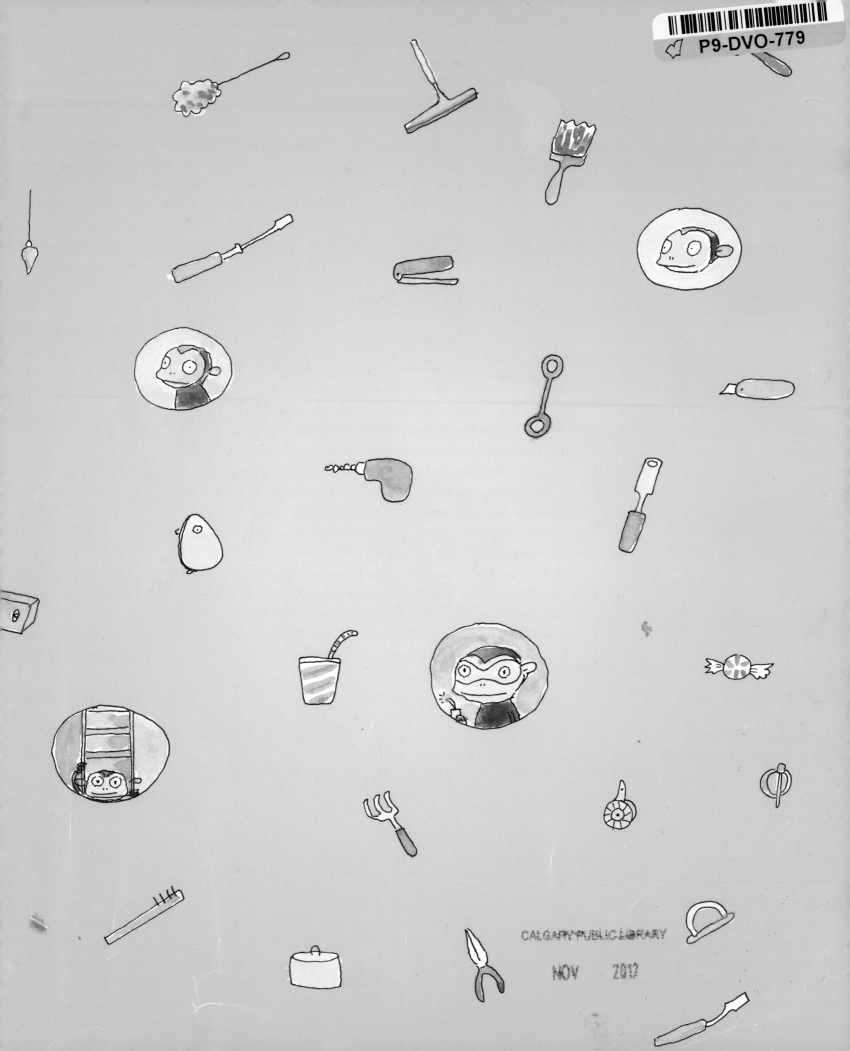

MONKEY WITH A TOOL BELT AND THE SILLY SCHOOL MYSTERY

Chris Monroe

CAROLRHODA BOOKS MINNEAPOLIS

For Barb

Carolrhoda Books
A division of Lerner Publishing Group, Inc.
241 First Avenue North
Minneapolis, MN 55401 USA

For reading levels and more information, look up this title at www.lernerbooks.com.

Design by Danielle Carnito.
Main body text set in Blockhead Unplugged 20/27. Typeface provided by Emigre, Inc.
The illustrations for this book were created in pencil on illustration board and then painted in gouache and inked.

Library of Congress Cataloging-in-Publication Data

Names: Monroe, Chris, author, illustrator.
Title: Monkey with a tool belt and the silly school mystery / written and illustrated by Chris Monroe.
Description: Minneapolis : Carolrhoda Books, [2017] | Summary: When school supplies go missing and suspicious bite marks appear, Chico the monkey (with his tool belt) investigates the mystery.
Identifiers: LCCN 2016042761 (print) | LCCN 2016058539 (ebook) | ISBN 9781512430103 (lb : alk. paper) | ISBN 9781512448566 (eb pdf)
Subjects: | CYAC: Tools—Fiction. | Schools—Fiction. | Monkeys—Fiction. | Animals—Fiction. | Mystery and detective stories.
Classification: LCC PZ7.M760 Moq 2017 (print) | LCC PZ7.M760 (ebook) | DDC [E]—dc23

LC record available at https://lccn.loc.gov/2016042761

Manufactured in the United States of America
1-41608-23513-1/6/2017

Chico Bon Bon and Clark
were on their way to school.

Chico wore a special tool belt for school.

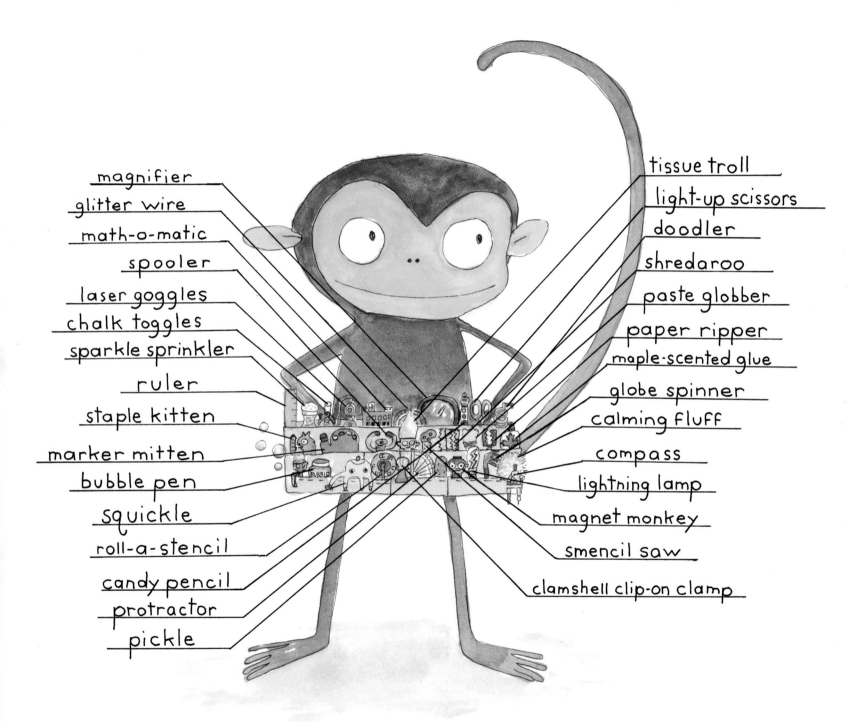

magnifier

glitter wire

math-o-matic

spooler

laser goggles

chalk toggles

sparkle sprinkler

ruler

staple kitten

marker mitten

bubble pen

squickle

roll-a-stencil

candy pencil

protractor

pickle

tissue troll

light-up scissors

doodler

shredaroo

paste globber

paper ripper

maple-scented glue

globe spinner

calming fluff

compass

lightning lamp

magnet monkey

smencil saw

clamshell clip-on clamp

His tools helped him with his class work...

and with all sorts of things that needed fixing.

They arrived right on time.

"Good Morning, everyone!" said Ms. Crabtree.
Chico and Clark took their seats.

Clark's chair
responded with
a noise that
sounded like
"CREEAAK . . . .
SPLAT,"

then broke into fourteen pieces.

Chico got out his chairepairer
and put it back together.

"Today we are going to the school library to pick out new books," Ms. Crabtree announced.

Chico had to repair a few things along the way:

He fixed a few lockers whose locks wouldn't lock.

He straightened the hands of the big hallway clock.

He oiled a door with an ear-splitting squeak

and fixed up the fountain— the one with the leak.

Mr. Marion, the librarian, welcomed the class.
But when he led them to the shelves,
he let out a quiet scream . . .

"Everything from *Aardvark Summer* to *Pygmy Pig's Pumpkin Patch* is gone!" he whispered loudly.

Maybe somebody is doing a really big book report," whispered Clark.

Chico looked unsure.

The students chose their books from the
letters Q through Z. Then they headed
back to their classroom for math class.

It was measuring day, but Ms. Crabtree could not find her ruler!

It's always right here!

Chico let her use the ruler from his tool belt.

The students measured different objects around the classroom.

Next, it was time for show and tell.

Clark was going to show his
watermelon (before snacking
on it later). But when he took
it out of his backpack,
half of it was gone!

Wayne took out his baseball
cards, but the whole team
had been chewed to pieces!!

Everybody's show and
tell things had problems.
It was a disaster.

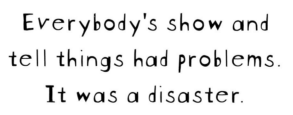

"Something strange is going on here," said Chico Bon Bon.

He slowly looked around the room.

Nothing seemed out of place.

Except for one thing.

There was an acorn on the pencil sharpener.

That's odd.

When the class headed outside for recess, Chico climbed
up the jungle gym and sat at the top, thinking.

What could be causing all of this? he wondered.

Was it:

Ghosts?

A magnetic field?

Sneaky gorillas?

A book club gone wild?

A prankster teacher?

Sixth graders?

Those girls over there digging a hole?

He just didn't know.

In geography class, they were studying the continents. But when Ms. Crabtree pulled down the map of North America, everything was missing except Canada!

Chico Bon Bon noticed tiny bite marks all along the Canadian border.

"This is definitely a clue, Ms. Crabtree," he said.

Just then the bell rang. It was time for lunch . . .

But when they got to the lunchroom, there were NO TACOS!

Someone had taken all the taco shells...
and the TRAYS!

"You'll have to put your taco fillings in these
paper cups," Lunch Lady Carol said sadly.
"Don't forget to grab a spork," she sighed.

Clark and Chico took their taco cups and sat down at a table. Chico filled a banana peel with his taco filling.

"This is almost as good as a shell," he said between bites.

"You sure are good with sporks," said Clark with his mouth full of lettuce.

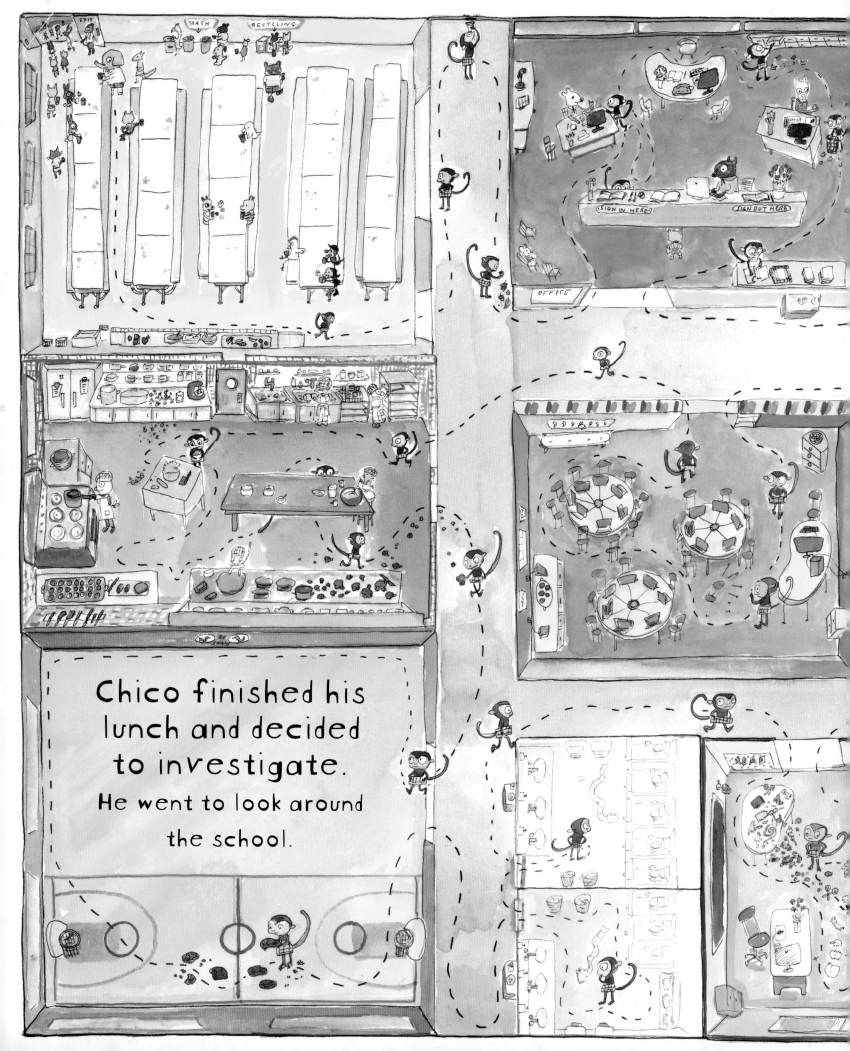

Chico finished his lunch and decided to investigate. He went to look around the school.

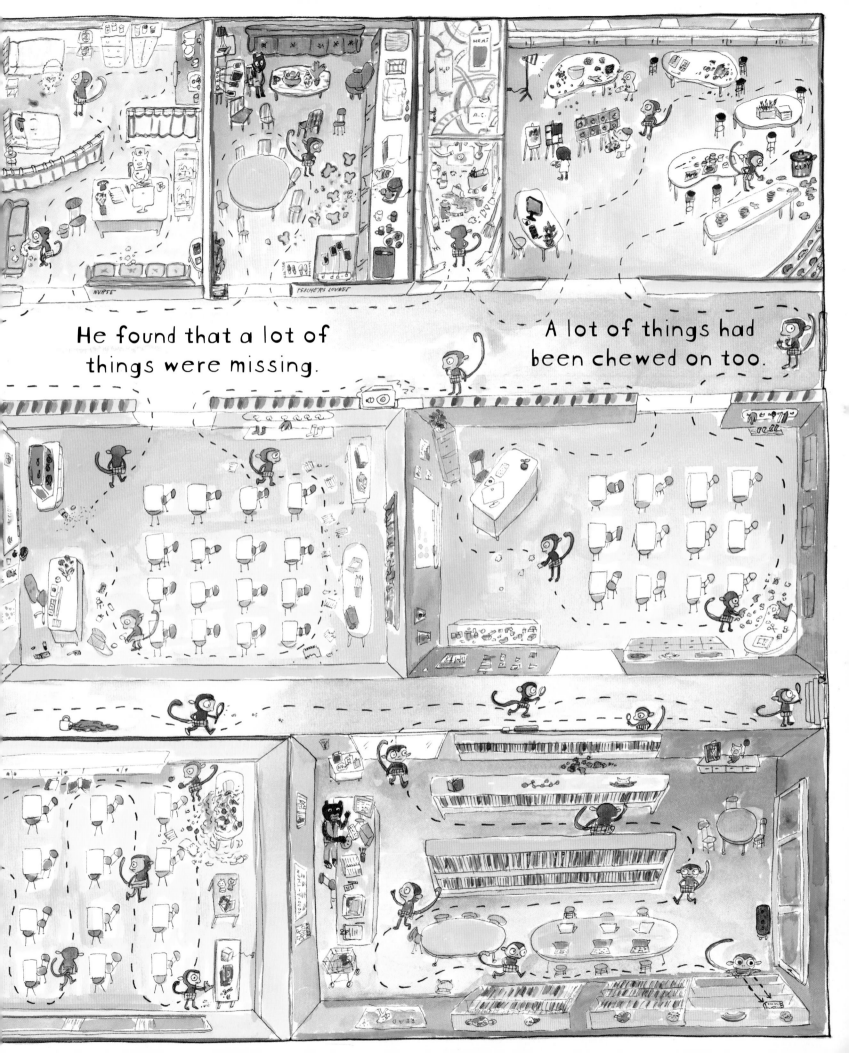

He found that a lot of things were missing.

A lot of things had been chewed on too.

In the library, he noticed there was still one book left on an empty shelf. He picked it up to take a closer look.

Behind the book, there was a hole in the wall!
Chico peered in and saw a tunnel. He heard
noises coming from somewhere inside.

He pulled out his flashlight and crawled in.

It was a room full of squirrels.
Squirrels had built a school in the walls.

The squirrels looked up when Chico popped
his head out of the tunnel.

Chico remembered a hollow oak tree by the playground. It would be perfect for a squirrel school.

So all the kids and squirrels helped him build it. Everyone shared Chico's tools.

Then Chico patched up the tunnel, and the squirrels returned all the stolen items.

When they had finished, they all
shared story time out on the lawn.
And even though the squirrels still may not
have been the ideal companions...

everybody
had fun.

"Boy, having your tool belt sure comes in handy at school," said Clark, tripping over a squirrel and crashing onto the seesaw.

"It really does!" said Chico as he reached into his tool belt for his clamshell clamps and super sticky seesaw sealant.

"For some reason, there's always something to fix!"

The End